CROC NEEDS TO WAIT

A book about PATIENCE

Written by Sue Graves

Illustrated by Trevor Dunton

Franklin Watts®
An imprint of Scholastic Inc.

Croc was very impatient. On the day of Giraffe's birthday party, Croc kept asking her mom if it was time to go yet. But her mom said she would just have to **be patient and wait**!

On Monday, Miss Bird asked everyone what they had done over the weekend. She said they had to take turns to speak.

But Croc was **too excited** to wait her turn. She **kept interrupting**. Miss Bird got upset. She said it was rude to interrupt someone when they were speaking.

During the math lesson, Miss Bird told everyone to add up their numbers carefully. She told them **not to rush**.

But Croc loved doing addition. She wanted
to see how fast she could get her work done.
She **forgot** to add carefully, and she got the
answers **all wrong**!

At recess it was raining. Everyone had to stay inside and play board games. Croc loved board games. But she got **too impatient** to wait her turn.

When it was Monkey's turn, Croc grabbed the dice instead. Worse still, she knocked over the board when she grabbed the dice. Everyone was upset with Croc for **ruining the game**.

After recess Miss Bird asked Croc and Hippo to color in a picture together. Hippo colored really carefully. He stayed inside the lines. But Croc was impatient to finish the picture. She didn't stay inside the lines at all.

Miss Bird said their picture **was not neat enough** to go on the wall. Hippo was upset. He said Croc should have been more patient.

The next day Miss Bird said the class was going to make flowerpots for their parents. She said the children must **make them carefully**. She said they must **wait** for the flowerpots **to dry** before painting them.

But Croc was so excited to be making a pot for her
mom that she didn't take her time. She **rushed**.
Her pot ended up being a very odd shape.

Croc **didn't wait** for the pot to dry before she painted it. All the paint ran off the pot and made a mess. Croc was sad.

Croc went to see Miss Bird. Miss Bird asked her what she should have done. Croc thought about it. She said she should have **taken her time**. She said she should have **been patient**. She said she should have waited for the pot to dry before she painted it.

Miss Bird said it was better to be patient and careful than to rush and ruin things. Croc said she would try to be patient in the future.

That afternoon Miss Bird said they were all going to make model boats to sail on the school pond. She said they had to work **in pairs**. Croc wanted to work with Hippo. Hippo was worried. He said Croc had to **work carefully**. Croc promised that she would.

Miss Bird gave everyone the instructions to read. She said they had to **take turns** to do each job.

Croc and Hippo worked really hard. Croc tried hard to be patient. She read the instructions carefully to Hippo.

She sorted the wooden shapes carefully.

She **waited patiently** while Hippo glued the shapes together.

They **both waited patiently** for the glue to dry.

Then Croc painted the boat. She **took her time** and painted it really well. She and Hippo waited for the paint to dry.

Last of all, Croc waited patiently while Hippo put the sail on the boat.

Everyone took their boats to the pond. All the boats sailed well. But Croc and Hippo's boat sailed the best of all. Croc was very pleased. She told Miss Bird that it was much better to be patient than to rush things and ruin them. Hippo said it was much nicer to work with someone who was patient!

A note about sharing this book

The **Behavior Matters** series has been developed to provide a starting point for further discussion on children's behavior both in relation to themselves and others. The series features animal characters reflecting typical behavior traits often seen in young children.

Croc Needs to Wait
This story looks at the importance of being patient and realizing that it is important to take time to do things carefully and to work cooperatively with others.

How to use the book
The book is designed for adults to share with an individual child or a group of children, and as a starting point for discussion.

The book also provides visual support and repeated words and phrases to build reading confidence.

Before reading the story
Choose a time to read when you and the children are relaxed and have time to share the story.

Spend time looking at the illustrations and talk about what the book might be about before reading it together.

Encourage children to tackle new words by sounding them out.

After reading, talk about the book with the children:

- Encourage the children to retell the events of the story in chronological order.

- Talk about Croc's impatience. Have the children felt impatient for their own birthdays to come around? Do they feel that time seems to pass too slowly when they are waiting for something exciting to happen?

- Discuss the importance of waiting their turn when others are speaking. Why should they not interrupt others? How do they feel if someone interrupts them when they are trying to explain something?

- Do the children think that Croc means to be rude or is her impatience often the result of being overexcited?

- Discuss the section of the story where Croc and Hippo work cooperatively to complete a task. Why is it important to work well with others? Can the children identify with this? Have they worked with a friend on a task? Invite them to share their experiences.

- Place the children into pairs. Provide a picture for each pair to color. Tell them they must decide which person will color each section. Remind them that they must work cooperatively and carefully to color the picture to the best of their abilities.

- Invite each pair to show their finished pictures to the others. Ask each pair how they decided who should color which section and why. Ask the children to talk about sharing a task with a friend. What did they particularly enjoy about it?

29

For Isabelle, William A, William G, George, Max, Emily, Leo, Caspar, Felix, Tabitha, Phoebe, and Harry —S.G.

Library of Congress Cataloging-in-Publication Data
Names: Graves, Sue, 1950– author. | Dunton, Trevor, illustrator.
Title: Croc needs to wait: a book about patience/written by Sue Graves; illustrated by
  Trevor Dunton.
Description: First edition. | New York: Franklin Watts, an imprint of Scholastic Inc., 2021. |
  Series: Behavior matters | Audience: Ages 4–7. | Audience: Grades K–1. | Summary: Croc
  always rushes ahead with whatever she is doing, whether it is waiting for her turn or doing her
  sums; frequently things go wrong, and projects are messed up—but when her teacher explains
  the importance of patience, Croc resolves to do better.
Identifiers: LCCN 2021000574 (print) | LCCN 2021000575 (ebook) | ISBN 9781338758047
  (library binding) | ISBN 9781338758054 (paperback) | ISBN 9781338758061 (ebook)
Subjects: LCSH: Patience—Juvenile fiction. | Crocodiles—Juvenile fiction. | Animals—Juvenile
  fiction. | CYAC: Patience—Fiction. | Crocodiles—Fiction. | Jungle animals—Fiction.
Classification: LCC PZ7.G7754 Cs 2021 (print) | LCC PZ7.G7754 (ebook) | DDC [E]—dc23
LC record available at https://lccn.loc.gov/2021000574
LC ebook record available at https://lccn.loc.gov/2021000575

10 9 8 7 6 5 4 3 2 1   22 23 24 25 26 27

Printed in China
First edition, 2022